Bunjitsu Bunny's Best Move

Bunjitsu Bunny's Best Move

Written and illustrated by
John Himmelman

Henry Holt and Company
New York

Henry Holt and Company, LLC
Publishers since 1866
175 Fifth Avenue, New York, New York 10010
mackids.com

Library of Congress Cataloging-in-Publication Data
Himmelman, John, author, illustrator.
[Short stories. Selections]
Bunjitsu Bunny's best move / John Himmelman. — First edition.
      pages   cm
Sequel to: Tales of Bunjitsu Bunny.
Summary: As Isabel, the best bunjitsu artist in her class, continues to practice her skills, she
also grows in her understanding of how to use her strongest weapon—her mind.
ISBN 978-0-8050-9971-3 (hardback) · ISBN 978-0-8050-9973-7 (e-book)
[1. Martial arts—Fiction. 2. Rabbits—Fiction. 3. Animals—Fiction.] I. Title.
   PZ7.H5686Bun 2015   [Fic]—dc23   2014047281

Henry Holt books may be purchased for business or promotional use. For information on bulk
purchases, please contact the Macmillan Corporate and Premium Sales Department at
(800) 221-7945 x5442 or by e-mail at specialmarkets@macmillan.com.

First Edition—2015
Printed in China by RR Donnelley Asia Printing Solutions Ltd.,
Dongguan City, Guangdong Province

1 3 5 7 9 10 8 6 4 2

For Sofia—
may your best move be one of many!

Contents

Isabel

Isabel was the best bunjitsu artist in her school. She could kick higher than anyone. She could hit harder than anyone. She could throw her classmates farther than anyone.

Some were frightened of her. But Isabel never hurt another creature, unless she had to.

"Bunjitsu is not just about kicking, hitting, and throwing," she said. "It is about finding ways NOT to kick, hit, and throw."

They called her Bunjitsu Bunny.

Shadows

One day, Isabel and her brother, Max, sat in a field. "Look at our shadows on the rock," said Isabel.

"Let's see how well they know bunjitsu," said Max. Max kicked his foot in the air. His shadow kicked its foot in the air. Isabel blocked the kick. Isabel's shadow blocked the kick.

"This is fun!" said Isabel.

Max's and Isabel's shadows
fought each other.

"My shadow has big teeth!" said
Max.

Isabel laughed. "My shadow has big antlers!" she said.

"My shadow has wings and can fly!" said Max.

"My shadow can tickle your shadow so it can't fly." Isabel laughed again.

Max moved away from the rock.
His shadow grew twice as large.
"Now you have to fight a giant
bear." Max's shadow pounded
Isabel's shadow with great big paws.
Isabel's shadow fell to the ground.

"My shadow has defeated the shadow of Bunjitsu Bunny!" said Max.

Isabel stood up and walked toward the rock.

"Now your shadow is like a little mouse," said Max.

"A quick little mouse," said Isabel.

Max's shadow tried to grab her shadow. Isabel's shadow darted away. Max's shadow tried to punch Isabel's shadow. Isabel's shadow darted away. Her little shadow was too quick for Max's shadow.

"I give up," said Max. "I thought being bigger and stronger would make me win."

"Sometimes," said Isabel. "But sometimes it's better to be a little mouse than a great big bear."

Bunjitsu Bunny Fails!

One morning, Teacher said, "Practice your bunchucks, class. Tomorrow I will test you to see how good you have become."

"You don't need to practice, Isabel," said Wendy. "You never fail."

On the day of the test, all the bunjitsu students gathered in the classroom.

Kyle went first. He swung his bunchucks so fast, no one could see them. Then he knocked the ball off its stand.

"Well done!" said Teacher. "You pass."

Then it was Betsy's turn. Her
bunchucks whistled in the air and
knocked the ball off its stand.

"That is the best you have ever
done!" said Teacher. "You pass."

All the students showed Teacher
what they could do. Each passed the
test.

Finally, it was Isabel's turn.

"This is a waste of time," said Ben. "Of course she will pass."

"It will still be fun to watch," said Wendy.

Isabel picked up her bunchucks.

"OW!" she said when one hit her ear.

"Ooch!" she said when they got tangled around her arm.

Then she tried to knock the ball off the stand.

"Strike one," whispered Ben.

"Strike two," whispered Betsy.

"Oh no! Strike three!" whispered Kyle.

"I am sorry, Isabel," said Teacher. "You did not pass the test, but I am sure you will next time."

Isabel was very sad. She had never failed before! Teacher asked her to stay after class.

"You should not be unhappy," said Teacher.

"But everyone passed the test except me," said Isabel.

"Do you know what you did wrong?" asked Teacher.

"Yes," said Isabel.

"Can you do better?" asked Teacher.

"Yes," said Isabel.

"Lucky you," said Teacher. "They passed the test, but you learned the most."

Mountain Goat

Isabel went for a hike on a chilly winter morning. At the end of the day, it was getting cold. She took a shortcut home and came to a bridge. Mountain Goat stood in the middle.

"Hi, Mountain Goat," said Isabel. "Would you please let me pass?"

"This is my bridge," said Mountain Goat. "You can pass if you beat my mighty horns."

"I do not want to bump heads with a goat," said Isabel.

"Then swim across the icy river," said Mountain Goat.

Isabel had little choice. She backed up and got a running start. Isabel and Mountain Goat met head-to-head.

CRASH! Isabel was knocked from the bridge.

She brushed herself off and backed up even farther. They met head-to-head.

CRASH! Isabel flew backward.

"Would you like to try again?" asked Mountain Goat.

She didn't want to try again. But she did want to go home. Isabel backed up farther yet. They met head-to-head.

CRASH! Isabel landed in a far-off tree.

"The great Bunjitsu Bunny cannot beat my mighty horns," shouted Mountain Goat, laughing.

He's right, thought Isabel. "One more try," she said.

"My pleasure," said Mountain Goat.

Isabel backed up half a mile. She ran so fast, her body was a blur. When she reached Mountain Goat, she leapfrogged over him!

"Hey!" shouted Mountain Goat. "We were supposed to bump heads!"

"I remembered what Teacher taught me," said Bunjitsu Bunny. "Don't let your enemy choose how you will fight."

Just DO It!

Four bunnies lay in the grass,
looking up at the sky.

"That cloud looks like my
grandma," said Ben. "I wish I was
at her house right now. I love my
grandma's hugs."

"Look at the cloud next to it,"
said Wendy. "It looks like a trumpet.
I wish I had my trumpet with me. I
love making music."

"That cloud makes me think of a
kicking bunny," said Max. "I really

should practice my bunjitsu kicks some more."

Isabel stood up and left.

"Where did she go?" asked Ben.

"You never know with her," said Max.

A few hours later, Isabel returned.
Her friends were still lying in the
grass.

"Where were you?" asked Wendy.

"Max made me think that I
should practice my bunjitsu kicks,

so I did. Wendy made me wish I
could go make music, so I did. And
Ben made me think of my grandma,
so I went and got a nice big
grandma hug."

The other three bunnies stood up.

"Where are you going?" asked
Isabel.

"You are right," said Ben. "Doing
something is better than talking
about it."

One Hundred Squirrels

Isabel loved to bake acorn cookies. She made a batch to give to her friends. As they were cooling, Squirrel showed up.

"Are those acorn cookies?" she asked.

"Yes," said Isabel. "I would give you one, but I made just enough for my friends."

"Then I will TAKE one!" said Squirrel. She reached for the cookies. Isabel chased her away. But when she turned around, Squirrel was back.

"COOKIES!" shouted Squirrel.

"No cookies," said Isabel, and she chased Squirrel off. When she turned around, Squirrel was heading for the cookies again.

"How are you doing that?" Isabel asked. She chased Squirrel away. When she got back, Squirrel was there.

"You can't be that fast!" said Isabel.

Then another squirrel appeared. And another. And another. Soon Bunjitsu Bunny had to defeat an army of one hundred cookie-loving squirrels.

She fought them one, two,
three, ten, fifty at a time. They kept
coming back.

I can't do this all day, thought Isabel. *But I will if I have to*. Then she had an idea. She held the tray over her head.

"The first one to get to these cookies can have them all," she said.

"COOKIES!" shouted the squirrels. They were so busy fighting one another, they didn't see Isabel tiptoe away with the tray.

The next day, Isabel baked more
acorn cookies. This time, she made
one hundred extra.

The Climb

Isabel wanted to climb to the top of Mount Snowcap. It was the tallest mountain in the area.

"That mountain is too big," said Max. "You will never make it to the top."

"I will try," said Isabel. She grabbed her backpack and headed up the mountain.

Climb. Climb. Climb.

Up. Up. Up.

Along the way, she came across a patch of pretty pink violets. She sat and drew pictures of them.

I'd better keep going, thought Isabel, *or I will never make it to the top.*

Climb. Climb. Climb.

Up. Up. Up.

"Hello," said a voice. "You look thirsty."

"Hello," said Isabel. "I am saving my water for when I get to the top."

"I am Snowshoe Hare. Come share some sweet mountain water with me."

Isabel and Snowshoe sat and talked. He had so many stories about living on the mountain.

"I'd better get going," said Isabel,
"or I will never make it to the top."

Climb. Climb. Climb.

Up. Up. Up.

A rock bounced down the hill. The sound echoed in the valley below.

"Hello," called Isabel.

"Hello hello hello," called her echo.

Isabel sang to the valley. The valley sang back to her. She was having so much fun, she lost track of time. Soon it would be dark. It was time to head down.

"Did you make it to the top?" asked Max when she returned home.

"No," said Isabel. "But that is okay. A goal can be something you aim for. What happens along the way makes it worth the try."

The Chore

One day, Teacher looked out at the garden behind the school. "There are so many weeds," he said. "Would any of you like to help get rid of them?"

All the students volunteered.

"I think it is a lesson he is teaching us," said Isabel. "Pulling weeds makes us practice the bunjitsu elbow strike."

"I think he wants us to dig them with our paws," said Ben. "It makes us practice the bunjitsu tornado block."

"No," said Kyle. "He wants us to use our feet to practice our bunjitsu kicks."

The bunnies spent the rest of
the day in the garden. They pulled.
They dug. They kicked. When they
were done, Teacher came outside.

"The garden looks wonderful," he said.

"And watch this," said Isabel. She showed Teacher her bunjitsu elbow strike.

"Good, good," said Teacher.

"Look at my bunjitsu tornado block," said Ben. His paws circled through the air.

"Beautiful," said Teacher.

"Watch THIS!" said Kyle. He
kicked mightily in the air.

"Very nice," said Teacher.

All the bunnies showed Teacher
what he'd had them practice.

"Those were good lessons you taught us," said Isabel.

"You taught yourselves those lessons," said Teacher.

"But isn't that why you wanted us to weed the garden?" she asked.

"No," said Teacher. "Sometimes the garden just needs to be weeded."

Lynx

Isabel was hopping home from school. Lynx blocked her path.

"So you are the great Bunjitsu Bunny," he said. "If I beat you in a fight, everyone will be afraid of ME!"

"I do not want to fight you," said Isabel.

"Too bad!" said Lynx. He leapt at Isabel. The two fought until she held him to the ground.

"Now it's over," said Isabel. "No more fighting."

The next day, Lynx was waiting
for her.

"I will beat you today," he said.
He leapt at the bunny. The two
fought until Isabel held him to the
ground.

"No more fighting," she said.

Lynx did not listen. Every day, he waited for Isabel. Every day, he fought her. Every day, he lost.

"I will keep fighting you until I win," said Lynx.

"Is there any way I can get you to stop?" asked Isabel.

"No one can make me do anything," said Lynx.

Isabel thought a moment.

"Okay," she said. "One more fight."

Lynx leapt at Isabel. The bunny fell to the ground.

"You win," she said. "I give up."

"I defeated Bunjitsu Bunny,"
he roared, and ran back into the
woods.

Kyle walked by. "Why did you let Lynx beat you?" he asked.

"I would rather lose one little fight," said Isabel, "than win a thousand of them."

Your Best Move

Bunjitsu class was over for the day.
"Before you go home," said Teacher,
"I want each of you to show me your
best way to stop a fight."

"I have a good one," said Betsy.
"Max, come and attack me."

Max ran at Betsy.

"WAHAA!" shouted Betsy. She
flipped Max through the air!

"My turn," said Max. "Betsy, come and attack me."

Betsy ran at Max.

"YAHEE!" shouted Max. He wrestled Betsy to the ground!

"I've got one," said Wendy. "Kyle, attack!"

Kyle leapt at Wendy.

"HEEYIP!" shouted Wendy. She pulled his ears!

"Watch this," said Kyle. "Wendy,
ATTACK!"

"HOOBAWOOBA!" shouted Kyle.
He spun and sent Wendy flying!

"Now it's my turn," said Ben.
"Isabel, ATTACK!"

Isabel grabbed Ben's shirt.

"HEEYA!" shouted Ben. He
yanked her to the ground!

When it was Isabel's turn, everyone backed up. They were all afraid to attack Bunjitsu Bunny.

"Be brave, my bunnies," said Teacher. No one stepped forward.

"Okay," said Betsy. "I will attack Isabel."

Betsy ran at Isabel.

Isabel wrapped her arms around Betsy and gave her a hug.

"This is my favorite way to stop a fight," she said.

"I'll attack her," said Wendy.

"No, me," said Max.

"No, I will," said Kyle.

"Next," said Ben.

"Nothing is more powerful than the bunjitsu hug," said Teacher with a laugh.

Mole Hole

Isabel liked to sit in her underground den. Her friend Mole often visited her. They sipped blueberry juice. They shared funny stories.

Sometimes they just sat quietly
and enjoyed being together.

One day, Mole looked sad.

"What is wrong?" asked Isabel.

"I always visit your den," said
Mole, "but you never visit mine."

"I would love to visit your den," said Isabel.

"Follow me," said Mole. He disappeared into his tunnel.

Mole's tunnel was very small.
Isabel barely squeezed through.
When she got to the end, she could
hardly move. She popped her head
into Mole's den.

"It is a very nice place," said
Isabel, "but I cannot fit inside."

"Oh," said Mole. "I did not think
of that."

He showed Isabel his favorite things. "This is a picture of my mom and dad."

"This is my comfy mushroom seat."

"This is the flute I like to play."

"I wish I could join you," said Isabel.

The next day, Isabel was very
busy. She drew a picture. She went
hunting in the damp forest. Then she
found a stick to carve.

"Come on over," she called to
Mole through his tunnel.

Mole came to Isabel's den.
Waiting inside was a comfy
mushroom seat, a flute, and a
picture of his mom and dad.

"That looks just like them!" said
Mole.

"Now my den is your den, too!"
said Isabel.

Mole perched on his comfy
mushroom seat and played a happy
tune.

Bzzzzz

Isabel watched Dragonfly zipping over a pond. "How did you learn to fly?" she asked.

"It is easy," said Dragonfly. "You just need four long wings and a long body."

Bzzzzz . . . Bumblebee buzzed
past.

"She doesn't have four long wings
and a long body," said Isabel.

b z z z z z

"Hmm," said Dragonfly.

Butterfly landed on a flower below. "You don't need four long wings and a long body," she said.

b z z z z z z z

"You need four WIDE wings and a TINY body."

Bzzzzz . . . Bumblebee buzzed by.

"She doesn't have four wide
wings and a tiny body," said Isabel.
"Hmm," said Butterfly.

Z Z Z Z Z Z Z Z Z Z Z Z Z

Raven landed on a branch above.
"You don't need four wide wings
and a tiny body," he said. "You need
TWO wings covered in FEATHERS."

Bzzzzz . . . Bumblebee buzzed
past.

"She doesn't have two wings covered in feathers," said Isabel.

"Hmm," said Raven.

Bzzzzz . . . Bumblebee buzzed back and forth between the reeds.

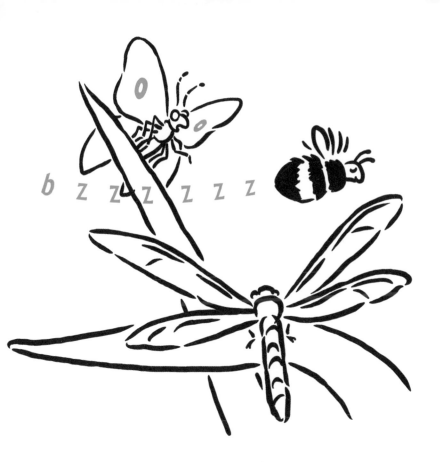

"That does not make sense," said
Dragonfly. "Bumblebee has very
short wings."

"And a large, round body," said
Butterfly.

"And no feathers," said Raven.

"You can't fly with short wings and a large, round body," they said.

"Maybe you can," said Isabel, "if you don't know you cannot."

Paper Bunny

Isabel and her friends were making paper animals.

Wendy made a paper goldfish.

Kyle made a paper bear.

Ben made a paper penguin.

Isabel made a paper mouse.

"Who can make a paper bunny?"
asked Wendy.

Ben folded a piece of paper. "No, this looks like a frog," he said.

Kyle folded a piece of paper. "This is a bunny with no ears," he said.

Wendy folded a piece of paper. "This is ears with no bunny," she said.

"Isabel," said Ben, "you are good at this. Will you show us how to make a paper bunny?"

"Yes," said Isabel. "But I can't show you now."

A week went by. "Can you show us how to make a paper bunny?" asked Wendy.

"Yes," said Isabel. "But I can't show you now."

Another week went by. "Now can you show us how to make a paper bunny?" asked Ben.

"Soon," said Isabel.

One month later, everyone was in Isabel's room. "NOW can you show us how to make a paper bunny?" they asked.

Isabel took out a piece of paper. Her paws moved quickly. Fold. Fold. Fold. Fold. Fold. Fold. She held up a perfect paper bunny!

"You did that so quickly! Why did you make us wait so long?" asked Wendy.

Isabel walked across her room
and opened her closet door. Out fell
hundreds of practice paper bunnies.

How to Make a Bunny Face

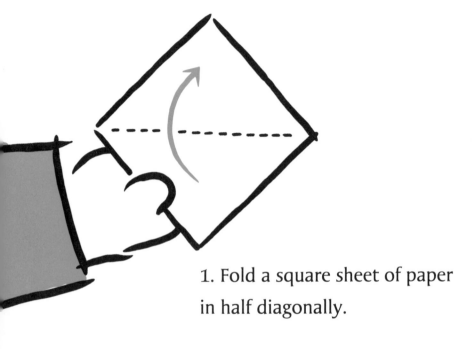

1. Fold a square sheet of paper in half diagonally.

2. Fold triangle in half, make a crease, and unfold.

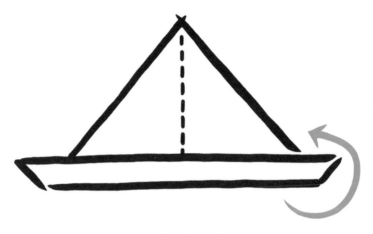

3. Fold up a little of the bottom.

4. Fold the
bottom corners
up to the crease.

5. Flip it over.

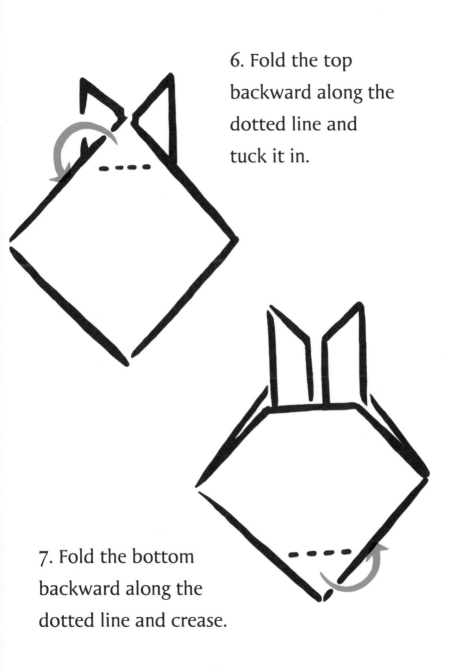

6. Fold the top backward along the dotted line and tuck it in.

7. Fold the bottom backward along the dotted line and crease.

8. Draw a bunny face!

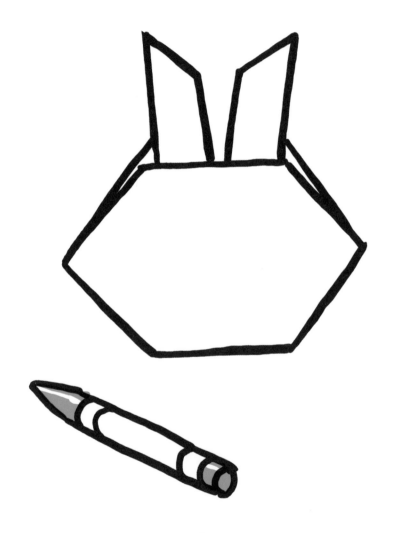

The Bunjitsu Code

All Bunjitsu students must do their best to follow the rules of Bunjitsu. If you wish to learn this art, you must read this and sign your name at the bottom.

I promise to:

- Practice my art until I am good at it. And then keep practicing.

- Never start a fight.

- Do all I can to avoid a fight.

- Help those who need me.

- Study the world.

- Learn from those who know more than I do.

- Share what I love.

- Find what makes me laugh, and laugh loudly. And often.

- Make someone smile every day.

- Keep my body strong and healthy.

- Try things that are hard for me to do.